Michael Hardcastle was born in Huddersfield in Yorkshire, and after leaving school he served in the Royal Army Educational Corps in England, Kenya and Mauritius. Later he worked for provincial daily newspapers in a variety of writing roles, from reporter and diarist to literary editor and chief feature writer.

He has written more than one hundred children's books since the first one was published in 1966, but he still finds time to visit schools and colleges all over Britain to talk about books and writing. In 1988 he was appointed an MBE in recognition of his services to children's books. He is married and lives in Beverley, near Hull.

OWN GOAL

Michael Hardcastle

illustrated by

Carol Binch

faber and faber

LONDON · BOSTON

First published in Great Britain in 1992
by Faber and Faber Limited
3 Queen Square London WC1N 3AU
This paperback edition first published in 1994

Printed and bound in Great Britain by
Mackays of Chatham PLC, Chatham, Kent
All rights reserved

A CIP record for this book is available
from the British Library

ISBN 0–571–17280–6

4 6 8 10 9 7 5 3

One

When the ball reached him from a well-taken corner kick Russell headed it against the cross-bar. William, the goalkeeper, failed to get a hand to the ball as it bounced around in the goalmouth. Someone else booted it clear, but gave away another corner kick at the same time.

'What were you *doing*?' William stormed at Russell. 'You almost scored for 'em there! So watch it.'

'Sorry.' Russell rolled his eyes upwards as if to show that's where he'd intended the ball to go. 'I won't do it again.'

'You'd better not,' William warned. He believed he should be the captain of Dorlin Tigers but the rest of the team said a goalie couldn't be a real leader because much of the time he was too far away from his own team-mates.

This time the corner kick wasn't so well aimed and William had no trouble in seizing the ball and throwing it straight to a team-mate. One day William was going to play for a top club. He'd set his heart on that and played every match as if his life depended on the result.

Russell was thankful the ball didn't come his way for several moments. He didn't feel very confident at present and Dorlin couldn't afford to lose another goal. They were already 0–1 down and there couldn't be more than five minutes still to play.

Tom, the skipper, was urging everyone to try harder, to go for the equalizer. 'We've got to get a point out of this match – and we can still win it,' he yelled as he lined up a free kick. Tom's Tigers the team was known as, but in this match they hadn't shown much bite. They were supposed to have sharp claws but a spectator remarked to a friend, 'They don't have claws and they don't have clues – clawless and clueless, that's what they are.' Fortunately, Tom didn't overhear that unkind remark.

Tom's trick free kick didn't work. His idea was to run up to the ball and then back-heel it to someone who would pass it out to the right for the winger to have a shot at goal. But the ref blew his whistle.

'The ball can't be passed backwards at a free kick,' he pointed out. 'You should learn the rules before you start playing any game. I'll let you off this time. You can have another go, just as long as you move the ball forward.'

Tom frowned. He didn't like it to be thought he didn't know what he was doing. And because he was annoyed with himself, the free kick was wasted. He hit the ball too hard, his friend Rupert couldn't control it and the Paxford team easily cleared the danger.

It was Dorlin's last chance to save the game. Within moments, Paxford were attacking again. Some Dorlin defenders chased back to keep Paxford out but others gave up because they were tired. Russell ran harder than anyone, eager to get in a vital tackle to make up for his earlier error. On the edge of the penalty area he overtook the player on the ball – Paxford's star, neat and skilful and very determined.

When Russell edged forward, as if preparing a tackle, the ginger-haired striker dallied with the ball, twisting as if to go one way, then turning to try another. Russell hesitated, but kept his eye on the ball as he'd been trained to do. Then, pushing the ball ahead of him, the Paxford boy darted towards goal at a speed that surprised Russell.

Keenly, Russell went after him. He must stop the striker getting a shot at goal. For a moment, the ginger-haired boy slowed down, lining up his shot. Russell pounced, foot-first, just as his opponent was shooting. The striker's aim was not good, but as the ball left his foot Russell's toe touched it – and the ball spun away, heading for the net.

William had rushed from his line, eager to shut down the attack. He should have shouted at Russell when he saw him about to make the tackle, but he didn't. Now, he had to watch, horrified, as the ball looped over his head and his clutching hands – and he knew without turning round that it would finish up in the back of the net. That was confirmed when the attacker wheeled away, punching the air with both fists to signal his joy at scoring.

William was furious. Furious with himself, but still more furious with Russell. Both boys knew the ball had gone into the net off Russell's toe. It was an own goal, the worst way of all for a team to lose a match.

Tom raced up to them, looking surprisingly calm after what had happened. 'Why did you do that?' he asked.

'Just tried to stop him,' Russell said, 'but he'd have scored anyway.'

'Rubbish!' William exploded. 'I had it covered. There's no way he'd have hit the ball past me. But Russell – Russell . . .'

Words failed him. He looked from Russell to

Tom and shook his head as if to say, 'This one's crazy.' Tom didn't look angry at all: just sad and rather baffled. He hardly ever made a stupid mistake himself, so he found it hard to understand that others were less skilful. Russell, guessing how his captain felt, just wanted to melt away, disappear from the game altogether. He was thankful that the final whistle would soon be heard.

'Honestly,' he said, thinking he had to say something, 'I could see he was going to score. It was obvious. I knew it as soon as he went past me.'

There was no time for further arguments. The referee was signalling impatiently for players to line up for the re-start and he looked at his watch twice. Paxford weren't bothered about scoring again; they just kept possession when the ball came to them, denying Dorlin any chance of a late consolation goal. In any case, most of the Dorlin Tigers had given up hope of saving the game. So it was relief all round when the final whistle shrilled.

Russell trudged from the pitch behind everyone else, thankful that none of his friends was among the handful of spectators. He'd kept quiet at home about this match, so he hadn't built up anyone's hopes of success. Normally his mother was quite interested in how he and the team got on, though some of her friends seemed surprised that he was as keen on football as he was on his computer. They didn't think the two things went together at all, but Russell couldn't see why they shouldn't.

Gareth, who'd missed a couple of easy scoring chances early in the game, moved across to sit beside him in the changing room. 'Wish I could score as easily as you did,' he remarked with a twisted sort of smile.

Russell glared at him. 'An own goal is not a joke, you know. I always play this game seriously. I desperately want us to win.' He yanked his black-and-yellow shirt over his head.

'Maybe we should change our colours,' Gareth continued, as if Russell hadn't spoken. He snapped at the waistband of his pale-green shorts. 'Green's unlucky, you know. My mum says if ever she wears anything green she's sure to suffer a disaster. She says that a lot.'

Russell, now changing his socks, thought that was a stupid comment and not worth a reply. Teams didn't change their colours in the middle of a season. And hardly at any other time either. He glanced round, expecting to see Tom or William coming towards him to tell him not to bother turning up for the next match. He was sure they'd drop

him, provided they could find a replacement. Dorlin, however, weren't well off for spare players.

'Want to come to my place before you go home?' Gareth asked. 'I've got a terrific World Cup video, got it for my birthday. We can see it together. You might get some ideas on how to be a top full-back.'

Russell was tempted. He didn't get many treats like that because his mum didn't approve of videos. She claimed there was quite enough electrical equipment around the house with Russell's computer and his dad's pile of disks.

'Well . . .' he started to say. Then he realized he was wearing a green sweater. Gareth's mother wouldn't like that at all; she'd probably not allow him into the house. 'No, can't,' he declared, standing up. 'Got to rush. Going to the shops with my nan. She wants to buy me a new coat, a top coat.'

'A *top* coat?' Gareth looked as amazed as he sounded.

'That's what she calls it,' Russell replied, picking up his bag. 'It's an anorak, really. See you, Gar.'

He grinned at escaping so easily; but the grin soon faded when he thought about his awful match. Maybe it would be his last game for Dorlin Tigers. Then he would be an ex-player. That sounded dreadful.

Two

'You look really glum,' Mr Kelly, their next-door neighbour, greeted him, his hands wet from the car he was washing in the drive.

'I *am* glum,' Russell told him grimly. 'I scored an own goal today.'

'Well, that sounds good to me, young Russ. Very, very good. It'd make me cheerful, I can tell you.' He squirted some soap on to the car's rear window.

Russell sighed. Mr Kelly was hopeless about football. 'No, it wouldn't cheer you up at all. You'd feel terrible, like me, if it happened to you. It's the very worst thing that can happen. It means you've scored for the *other* side. Terrible.'

'Oh, I see.' Mr Kelly looked glum now. But he held out the soap gun to Russell. 'Want a squirt?'

'Thanks.' Russell aimed the gun at a headlamp – and hit it spot-on. That cheered him up a bit. He aimed at the other lamp – and hit that, too.

Mr Kelly smiled. 'Well, that proves you're a

smart shot. Nothing wrong with your shooting at all. You can clean my car any time you like.'

'I'd rather play football, as long as I'm being a proper defender. When I tackle someone and take the ball off him and then hit a long pass to one of our players, it feels like, well, the best thing in the world. Even better than winning six of my computer games in succession – you know, a double hat-trick. That's what I call it, anyway.'

Russell suspected that Mr Kelly didn't really know what he was talking about but probably that didn't matter. The old man had been listening intently.

'What do you think went wrong today, Russ?' he asked, picking up a polishing cloth to start shining up the bonnet. Russell's dad said that Mr Kelly's car was as good as a mirror.

'Don't know,' Russell admitted. 'I mean, I could see their striker was going to score, so I wanted to stop him. But I'll have to think about it properly. I mustn't make another mistake like that. They'll kick me out of the team if I do.'

Mr Kelly shook his head sadly. 'Look, young Russ, mistakes like that ain't worth bothering about. Best forgotten. If you think about 'em too much, you'll make the same mistake again. Bound to, believe me.' He fished in a pocket and held out a key. 'Forgot to say, your mum's had to go out. Told me to tell you she'll be back in plenty of time to make your tea. You're to tidy your room before your nan comes.' Mr Kelly chuckled. 'I think that's an order. But you can come and have a cup of tea with us first, if you fancy one.'

'No, thanks,' said Russell, not wanting to be fussed over by Mrs Kelly, who always asked babyish questions. 'I'd better get on with my room if Mum says I've got to do it. Then I might get a new computer game from Nan instead of a boring old anorak. See you, Mr Kelly.'

As he let himself into the house, he heard the phone ringing. He thought it might be his mother, checking whether he was home, so he decided to answer it. The call was for him but it wasn't from his mother.

'Hi, Russ, how you doing?' enquired his best friend, Angelo, who never announced his name when telephoning. But he didn't really need to – Russell didn't know anyone else who had such a mixture of accents or who was always so cheerful. 'Look, how'd you like to come over right now and play a game of chess?'

'Can't. Got to tidy my room. Mum's orders.

Then we're going out to get me a new anorak.'

Angelo wasn't put off. 'It's my dad wants to play you. He says you're the best for your age he's ever met. How'd you think that makes me feel?'

Russell smiled. He knew Angelo wasn't really upset; he just liked to exaggerate. Russell quite liked playing his friend at chess but it was a bit boring because Russell nearly always won. He hadn't beaten Mr Coletta very often, so he was tempted.

'My dad says he doesn't know *anyone* who thinks as far ahead as you do,' Angelo went on. 'But he says he's got you worked out now. Knows how to beat you in double fast time. So if you win, he'll give you a *triple* helping of your favourite pasta dish. How can you turn that down, Russ?'

Russell licked his lips. In his opinion, Mr Coletta made the best food in the world, which was why his Italian restaurant was always so popular. It was called Pasta Perfetta.

'Bet you're feeling starved right now, just thinking about it!' Angelo pressed on. 'Right?'

It was true. Russell couldn't deny it. But he wasn't going to admit it. 'Sorry, Angelo, but I just can't get away. I've got a job to do for my mum and I've just come in from playing football. So – '

'Football! That stupid game! Why waste your time on football, Russ?'

'I like it.' There was nothing else to say – except, perhaps, that he did more than like the game: he loved it. But Angelo seemed unable to understand that, which was odd for an Italian boy. Still, Angelo had spent his early years in America, where soccer wasn't so popular. 'Look, I'll come and play your dad another time, Angelo, I promise. I mean, I'd like a *triple* helping of green pasta with mushrooms and tomatoes in a creamy cheese sauce and –'

'OK, OK, you got it – when you come and win,' Angelo cut in. 'Gotta go now. See you, Russell.'

Russell sighed and put down the receiver. This was turning out to be one of the worst days of his life, scoring an own goal and missing out on a marvellous meal (he had no doubt at all that he'd beat Mr Coletta again at chess). Then he'd probably have to accept a new anorak when all he wanted was a new computer game because he'd mastered all the games he already had. *And* he was supposed to tidy his room when it was perfect as it was. There was nothing strewn about and he knew precisely where everything was. This was just his mother's way of getting at him for being clever.

People kept telling him he was clever but he

thought they weren't always pleased about it. Sometimes they said he was too clever for his own good, whatever that meant. But he knew he wasn't clever at everything: football, for instance. He made lots of mistakes at football, and he couldn't understand why. So that must prove he wasn't as clever as some believed.

He wished Angelo knew about football, because then they could talk about it together and probably work out what Russell was doing wrong. He could learn the right way to play. He wanted to be as good at football as he was at computer games, chess and mental arithmetic. Russell could do lots of things other people found impossible – so surely he could learn to be a top footballer, like William or Tom. After all, they weren't brilliant at school subjects. There *must* be ways to learn . . .

That thought was in his mind as he looked round his perfectly tidy room. And then he remembered Gareth's offer to share his World Cup video with him so they could 'pick up some tips' on how to play better. Really, it wasn't a bad idea. Maybe he should phone Gareth and say he'd go round as soon as possible. But first, he'd better change out of the green sweater.

He was heading for the phone in the kitchen

when the door opened and his mother, weighed down with shopping bags, walked in. When she noticed him she smiled, gave a lurch of mock exhaustion and said, 'Be thankful you don't have to do all this shopping. It's wearing me out.'

'But you don't have to do it all in one go,' Russell pointed out, politely taking a bag from her and starting to empty the contents on to the table. 'If you spread it out over the week, it'd be much easier. Look, I'll do a plan for you, if you like. You know, which day to go to which shop and what to get then and –'

'Not on your life!' his mother cut in. 'I don't want to drag this out all week, so I can do without one of your master plans, thank you very much! At least now I don't have to go off again for another seven days – well, five maybe. Oh, I've got some news for you. Your nan's not coming round this evening. She's not at her best. She's complaining of funny twinges in her legs. We might nip round and see her instead. She can decide what to do about your anorak – sorry, *top coat* – then. OK?'

'OK.' Russell nodded. He was calculating that now it might be possible to persuade his nan to buy him a new computer game – or at least something more useful than a boring old coat. 'Er, Mum, if you don't need my help in the pantry I'll go and, er, sort out my room. Maybe I could organize it a bit better.' He smiled winningly.

Mrs Baillie's look was one of amazement. 'Miracles,' she murmured, 'sometimes happen!'

Three

Russell leaned forward on the sofa, his eyes alight with delight. 'Hey, that was great!' he exclaimed. 'Can we see that bit again? Can you stop the video and run it back a bit?'

Gareth frowned. 'But there's a good goal coming up right now. I want to see what that German striker did before he hit the ball into the net. You know, how he beat that American full-back on the edge of the penalty area. That bit's magic.'

Russell bit his lip to prevent himself saying a word. It was Gareth's video, so he was entitled to play it as he liked, but all he wanted to see was the strikers in action. It didn't matter to him what the defenders did.

The film ran on and Gareth almost swooned with pleasure when his German hero performed his clever tricks.

'Now, which bit was it you wanted?' he asked when, at last, he'd seen it often enough.

'The Scotland–Sweden game, that fantastic over-

head kick by the full-back. What a way to clear a ball! It must be great to be able to do that.'

'It's called a bicycle kick,' said Gareth, punching buttons on his remote control to catch the right bit of film. 'Looks spectacular. But it's very hard to do properly.'

Russell blinked. 'How d'you know that?'

Gareth stopped the film, frowning again. 'It's obvious. Doesn't it *look* sort of impossible?'

'No, no, I can see that. I mean, who told you it's called the bicycle kick?'

'I thought *everybody* knew that.' Gareth was astonished to discover he knew something that Russell didn't. 'That's the way it looks, isn't it, if you think of the player the other way up – as if he were riding a bicycle.'

Russell could see that now, although he rather wished Gareth's video machine were smart enough to play a film upside down when you needed it; already he was imagining how wonderful it would be to kick a ball in that way. That would really make up for his own goal against Paxford.

'Oh, let's see it again – just once more, Gareth, please!' he pleaded. Gareth gave in. He didn't have many friends, so he didn't want to lose Russell's companionship, but before he'd got the picture he wanted, his mother walked in.

'Goodness, is this all you can think to do, watch TV?' she exclaimed. 'You should be out doing something healthy – fresh air and exercise, that's what you need.'

'I agree,' Russell said immediately, to Gareth's surprise. 'We can go and practise bicycle kicks. Come on, Gar.'

'*Gareth*, if you don't mind,' Mrs Oliver said heavily. 'I didn't give him a lovely name like that to have it *mangled*. Please remember that.'

'Sorry,' Russell muttered. He found it hard to look at her because she was large and rather fierce.

Her gaze shifted to his feet. 'Oh, my goodness!' she exclaimed, rolling her eyes back into her head. 'Green socks! Take them off at once. They're polluting the house with bad luck.'

'What?' Russell was staggered. There was hardly any green at all in his socks, just a tiny fleck here and there among the reds and browns. 'But . . .'

'Take them off at once!' Mrs Oliver ordered. 'Gareth, go and fetch him a pair of yours. Really, you ought to know better than to allow a friend of yours into this house wearing that dreadful colour.'

Gareth dashed away obediently while Russell

stripped off his socks, thinking that it was a good thing he wasn't wearing green trousers. He didn't care for the idea of putting on someone else's socks, but he had no option – it wasn't warm enough to go out barefoot. The pair Gareth provided was in a ghastly shade of pink. Russell shuddered as he pulled them on. It was so stupid, because moments later the boys were out of the house and out of Mrs Oliver's sight.

'Sorry about that,' Gareth mumbled. 'Didn't think she'd notice.'

Russell was going to make the most of his teammate's apology. 'Right then,' he said briskly, 'you can whack a few crosses over to me so that I can practise that trick kick. Hey, that's good! Trick kick.'

Gareth didn't think much of that idea; he wanted to get in some shooting practice. But after the business of the socks he supposed he ought to do what Russell demanded. Collecting a football from the shed at the bottom of the long, narrow garden, he led the way over a low fence on to some common land dotted with tangled bushes and, surprisingly, a set of deeply rusted goalposts. Gareth had rigged up an old clothes line to act as a cross-bar, but he wished there was a net as well.

21

'Oh, great, just right for soccer training,' Russell remarked. 'I haven't got anything as good as this where I live. Have to sneak on to the pitch at my school when I can – and when the caretaker isn't looking. Doesn't seem to like me for some reason.'

He stationed himself by the penalty spot, facing the posts, and waited for the first waist-high cross. It took Gareth a few goes before he sent the ball over at the right height – and then Russell missed it completely. In falling, he landed flat on his back, which knocked the breath out of him, but, with the turf softened by recent rain, he suffered no damage.

'You missed it by a mile!' Gareth scoffed. 'You took off before the ball even got near you. You're hopeless!'

'Look, it was the wrong height, that's all,' Russell protested. 'Try it again.'

'OK, it's your funeral.' Gareth was quoting a phrase his mother used when someone was being foolish.

Again it took a few attempts before Gareth sent over the sort of cross Russell could go for – and this time the kicker got his foot to the ball. But it was his toe, not the instep, that made contact. So instead of hooking the ball cleverly over his head Russell simply diverted it between the posts.

'Fantastic!' Gareth mocked. '*Another* own goal. Tiger Tom's going to be wild about this trick, Russell.'

Russell grunted. He'd been sure he was going to get it right that time. His timing should have been perfect: he took off just before the ball was going to reach him. Yet he scored an own goal instead of clearing the ball way out of the penalty area in the other direction. It just wasn't fair. He couldn't imagine what was wrong.

'That's it,' Gareth said, lining up a shot at goal for himself.

'No, come on, Gar, one more, just *one*,' Russell pleaded. Then he spotted another boy, hovering by one of the big bushes at the side of the old pitch. He looked as though he wanted to join in but daren't ask.

'Who's that?' he asked Gareth, who just shrugged, shook his head and replied, 'No idea. Who cares?'

Russell cared. Another player might send over better crosses than Gareth had managed.

'Want a game?' Russell called. To make the invitation as positive as possible, he booted the ball towards the boy in the red sweater and black

trousers. Without saying a word, he brought the ball down, then cleverly flicked it up again and, with his left foot, volleyed it between the posts.

'I can see you've never kicked a ball before in your life.' Russell said with a smile, while Gareth just frowned. 'What's your name? D'you live around here?'

'Just moved from London, so I don't know anybody around here,' was the answer. 'My name's Jordan and I know it's different but *I* like it, OK?'

'OK, no problem, Jordan. I'm Russell and he's Gareth. Look, I'm practising bicycle kicks because I want to be good at them. So if – '

'I watched you,' Jordan cut in. 'But you're jumping in too fast. You've got to time it right, otherwise you'll just mis-kick like you've been doing.'

'Oh, I didn't realize that,' Russell said, grateful for the observation. It made him realize how keenly Jordan must have been watching them. 'Perhaps I could get it right next time if you whipped a cross over for me at the right height.'

Jordan darted away to retrieve the ball from under a bush behind the posts. So far Gareth hadn't said a word and Russell sensed he wasn't pleased to have another player join them.

'Did you play for a team in London, then?' Russell asked.

'Yeah, two teams, actually, one Saturday, one Sunday. I'm a striker. I got plenty of goals for both teams. Our coach at Dalston said I had the knack of being in the right place at the right time to shoot 'em in.'

'Look, let's get on with playing,' Gareth said. 'I've got to go in soon and it's my ball.'

Russell and Jordan exchanged looks but didn't voice their thoughts. Instead, Jordan said briskly, 'Right, get yourself in position and I'll put the ball over. But don't go for it too soon, OK?'

'I won't,' Russell insisted, determined to get it right this time.

It was at the perfect height and Russell, watching it all the way, timed it beautifully, hooking his right foot round the ball and directing it between the posts just below the point where the crossbar would have been.

'Well done, great shot!' Jordan yelled. But then, seeing the pain on Russell's face as he attempted to get to his feet, he darted across to help the goal-scorer. 'What's up? Is it your shoulder?'

'Yeah,' Russell gasped, biting his lip. 'Must have

landed on it – and my elbow really hurts too. Ouch!' He tried to massage the affected area but stabbing pain was the only result. Yet he could still think about the brilliant goal he'd scored. Then it struck him: he'd faced the wrong way! He should have been trying to clear the cross, not score from it. Jordan, not realizing what Russell was attempting to do, had delivered the ball while Russell was facing the wrong way, and, instinctively, Russell had gone for it. Still, it proved he *could* perform the bicycle trick.

'You can't have broken a bone, otherwise the bits would probably be sticking out through the skin,' Jordan remarked in a very matter-of-fact way. 'Saw that happen in one of our London matches and the kid just fainted from shock when he saw what he'd done.'

Gareth suddenly paled, looking as if he might be sick at any moment. Having collected the ball, he was bouncing it furiously on the spot. 'Look, I've got to be off. We can train another time.'

Tucking the ball under his arm, he turned away, but then he remembered something: 'Oh, yes, I'll need those socks, Russ. My mum'll want to wash 'em. Can you change into your own? You've got them in your pocket, haven't you?'

Russell was still in too much discomfort to pro-
test. It was a bit awkward, trying to remove them
without doing further injury to his damaged
shoulder but, after sitting down, he managed it. He
was thankful neither of them offered to help: that
would have made him feel worse. Jordan watched
silently and only made a one-word comment when
Gareth had departed: 'Weird!'

Russell explained about the fear of green as an
unlucky colour. Jordan shook his head, even more
surprised. 'Didn't do us any harm at Dalston when
we played in green shirts. Actually, we won the
League, so green must've been good for us when
you think about it. Look, Russell, come over to my
place. We can bring one of my footballs back here
later if your shoulder's OK. My mum's a nurse, so
she'll have a look at it if you like. She also makes a
great chocolate cake and she was baking last night.
OK?'

'Great,' replied Russell, thankful for a chance to
rest his shoulder. Although the pain was easing he
didn't want to move his arm much for fear of
making things worse.

Jordan's home was bigger than Gareth's and a
couple of packing cases were still in the hall. Mrs
Hall was practically the opposite of Gareth's

mother: tall, thin, cheerful and very welcoming. She broke off from washing cupboard shelves to make the boys a drink, cut them generous slices of cake and examine Russell's injuries. Her fingers probed carefully but nearly painlessly.

'Nothing broken, I'm sure,' she reported. 'You could have tugged a muscle and you'll definitely have bruises. But if you don't swing your arm for a day or so I'm sure you'll be fine, Russell.'

She smiled comfortingly. 'Now, why don't you boys go and watch a cartoon or something and leave me to my cleaning? Feel free to come round whenever you like, Russell. Jordan hasn't had time to make any friends in Dorlin yet.'

'I've got a better idea,' Jordan confided when they were on their own. 'Come and see my collection of football programmes. I'm still deciding where to put them. My dad's just got me one of the World Cup semi-final programmes. It's terrific.'

'So's this cake,' Russell reported. 'What's your Dad do, then?'

'He's in the travel business – that's why he keeps going off on long trips to Italy and America and places like that. He's promised me he'll take me to America next time he goes. Can't wait.'

Jordan's room was twice the size of Russell's,

30

with cupboards big enough for people to hide in. Looking round, Russell said, 'You haven't got a computer, then?'

'No, thanks,' Jordan replied. 'I want to do things, not play at them.'

Russell made no response to that. Soon he was absorbed in the huge collection of programmes and signed photos of top players in Germany and Italy as well as in England and Scotland. Two pictures of a tall, blond striker in the German League were inscribed 'To Jordan, Best of luck. Wolfgang.'

'He's the greatest,' Jordan said. 'I want to score as many goals as him when I get to the top. My dad actually knows him. He's done work for my dad's firm, promoting Bavaria, where he lives.'

'Do you always play as a striker?' Russell asked.

'Normally, yes. Sometimes on the wing, too, if a team's got plenty of good forwards. Listen, does the team you and Gareth play for need a striker?'

'Desperately,' said Russell solemnly, echoing one of Tiger Tom's favourite words. 'If you can score goals, Tom – he's our captain – will, well, give you his spare boots or something.'

Jordan smiled. 'I think I've got enough boots of my own. But there is a problem if I am to play for your team. My eyes are green. I can't change them like a pair of socks.'

For a moment Russell was puzzled. Then he saw what Jordan meant. 'Oh, that's just Gareth, with his funny ideas about unlucky green. Nobody else worries like that. Anyway, if you play for us, he'll be the one you replace, probably. Gareth's pretty useless at scoring goals.'

'So, when's your next match?'

'Sunday, against Surfleet. We really need to beat them to get up the League. I'm sure Tom'll want you to play. Certain to.'

It was only when he was making his way home, supporting his left elbow as best he could, that Russell remembered that his own place in the team was far from certain.

Four

Surfleet were among the top teams in the League and they were already out on the pitch, training eagerly, when most of the Dorlin Tigers turned up at their Edge Lane ground. Jordan, arriving with Russell, studied their opponents, whose red-and-white strip looked as if it had all come out of the same laundry that morning.

'The way they're going at it they'll be worn out by half-time,' he remarked. 'I should get some goals in the second half.'

Russell didn't reply. He wasn't at all sure that Tom would be willing to play Jordan in the team. When Russell phoned him, Dorlin's skipper wasn't in the mood to say much at all; Russell sensed he was still angry with him for that own goal against Paxford. Russell suspected that Tom might have doubts about Jordan simply because he, Russell, was recommending him. Perhaps Gareth's opinion would be helpful, unless Gareth felt threatened by Jordan's arrival on the scene. Real life, Russell had decided, threw up more problems than his computer. On top of everything, Tom had refused to promise that Russell himself would be in the team.

William, however, seemed to be in no doubt that Russell was playing. 'Better not score any more goals against us today,' he said menacingly to Russell in the changing room. 'If you do, you'll be out for good. Never play for the Tigers again.'

'This is Jordan Hall,' Russell said to William, trying to ignore the threat. 'He's new here but he played as a striker in London and got tons of goals.'

'Did he tell you what he did last week?' William asked Jordan. 'Scored a goal *against* us, just when I had the shot covered. Unbelievable!'

'Even the England captain mis-hits a shot sometimes. No one's perfect,' Jordan replied mildly. Russell felt wonderfully cheered by that support. No one else had stood up for him. 'Anyway, it's not the sort of thing you do every match, is it, scoring an own goal?'

'Better not be,' William remarked darkly.

Russell wished he played for a top club where a team sheet was pinned up in the changing room by the manager to let everyone know as soon as they arrived who was playing. But the Dorlin players had to await the arrival of the captain, the only selector. Russell hadn't mentioned his shoulder injury on the telephone because he wasn't going to provide Tom with an easy excuse to drop him. In any case, there was only the teeniest twinge of pain when he shrugged his shoulder or moved it sharply.

When Tom arrived, Gareth was with him, and Russell suspected that meant Tom would now know all about their training session when Russell managed only one success with his bicycle kicks. To his surprise, however, Tom came straight across to Jordan as if he'd always known him.

'You can play for us if you want,' he announced. 'Matthew's got some stupid band practice, so he can't get away at the usual time. I've told him he'll be one of the subs when he turns up. You can play up front with me and score some goals if you can.'

'OK,' replied Jordan, accepting a spare Tigers' shirt that Tom always carried in his sports bag. And that was all that was said about his place in the team. Russell didn't get more than a glance. It was as if Tom simply accepted that he was there and would be playing as usual.

The captain's message to his side before they went out to play was also simple, and brief: 'We've got to beat this lot. We need the points badly. Good luck.'

'And no stupid mistakes,' added William unnecessarily, giving Russell a warning glance.

It wasn't until he changed that Russell saw how thin Jordan was; but his speed when he sprinted on to the pitch was electric. Suddenly Russell realized that he might be just the player the Tigers needed. And if he turned out to be a regular goal-grabber, the team would surely be grateful to the person who'd found him.

Gareth still hadn't said a word to Russell and it appeared that the only person he was interested in now was Tom, not only his co-striker but his captain. Gareth was aware that if he had another poor

game it might be his last for Dorlin Tigers, especially now that a new player with a reputation for scoring goals was in the side. Unlike Tom, Gareth had always played more for himself than for the team.

Surfleet, with the confidence of a string of good results behind them, attacked from the start. One of their mid-fielders, a boy so round that he seemed almost as wide as he was tall, attracted the ball like a magnet. He sprayed accurate, clever passes to their front-runners wherever they were, on the wing or in mid-field. He was known to his team-mates as 'The Tyre Man', or just 'Tyre'. Never still for a moment, he seemed to have endless energy.

It was one of his passes that nearly brought the first goal. With brilliant timing, he floated the ball over the heads of several players to one of his strikers on the edge of the box, who turned quickly as he brought the ball under control.

The Dorlin full-back's attempt at a tackle was clumsy and thus easily avoided. The route to goal was clear – except for William's presence. And William didn't hesitate to advance, ready to dive and spread his body to prevent a goal. For a moment the striker dallied, trying to decide which way to go round the goalie. And because he took his eye off the ball he lost control of it as he veered to the left. William pounced but, with the ball spinning awkwardly, he couldn't hold it. Before the striker could recover possession Russell darted across to hook the ball to safety.

'Great save, William!' he called to the Tigers' keeper. And from mid-field Tom, too, signalled congratulations. The last thing Dorlin wanted was to concede an early goal.

That disappointment, however, made Surfleet all the keener to put themselves in front and for the next few minutes the Dorlin goal was under siege, Tom dropping back to help out. Tyre was still in control, stabbing or rolling or lobbing pinpoint passes to players in a position to go forward or try a shot. Surprisingly, Tom hadn't thought to put a marker on the Surfleet dynamo. But then, he and his fellow defenders were actually coping quite well with the problems they were facing . . . and Surfleet still hadn't got the ball in the net.

Russell was getting through a lot of work and, so far, he hadn't put a foot wrong. Then, as his confidence increased, he couldn't resist trying out his new trick when, unexpectedly, the ball was sent flashing across the face of the goal by a Surfleet winger. At that moment Russell was turning towards the net and so there was no risk he would kick the wrong way – at least, that was what he thought in the split second he had to make up his mind.

Jump – going high – reach out with one foot – lean back, make contact with the ball – fall, fall, fall – land heavily. Crash!

There didn't seem to be any breath in his body. For some moments, he couldn't even get up. He had no idea where the ball was. He just knew it hadn't flown back over his head as he'd intended.

Nobody went to his aid as players surged around him, several trying to head the ball that had flown high into the air, straight up like a rocket from the toe of Russell's boot. Then William charged out, leapt and, with his left fist, knocked the ball away. The clearance was completed by Tom, belting the ball upfield with all the strength he could muster.

Russell struggled to his feet just as an anxious referee ran up to him. 'OK now, son?' the man wanted to know.

Russell nodded, still unable to speak. He was winded but he didn't mind that because he hadn't done any further damage to his elbow. That felt fine.

William, retreating to his goalmouth, glared at him. 'What were you trying to do? You must be mad, kicking like that.'

Russell was as furious with himself as William was furious with him. He knew even as he climbed into the air that he was going to mis-time his kick. The ball wasn't coming to him quite as fast as he'd expected. That was why he had made a hash of it. He'd been desperately keen to try out the bicycle kick – but he'd chosen the wrong moment for it. Still, at least he hadn't scored another own goal.

Tom hadn't said a word to him but there wasn't time for one. Dorlin, after being penned in their own half for so long, were on the attack.

Tom's clearance had sent the ball far up-field, where it was pushed out to Gareth. And Gareth did exactly the right thing: he hit a first-time pass for Jordan to run on to. And Jordan ran, ran like an Olympic sprinter, head down and determined to leave everyone well behind him.

Because their side had been on the attack for so long, Surfleet's defence was spread out. Sensing danger, their goalkeeper crept forward, trying to decide what to do for the best. But nothing and no one was going to stop Jordan in full flight. Dorlin's new striker swerved to the left past one defender, swerved to the right past the flailing keeper – and coolly slid the ball into the net.

'Fantastic!' yelled the usually calm Tom, rushing to greet his goal-scorer. It was a long time since Dorlin had taken the lead against a top team.

Two minutes later the Tigers were two up. Surfleet, unable to believe they were losing, had rushed into attack, sending almost everyone up-field in search of the equalizer. But when the ball ran loose Russell took it with him for a few strides before hitting a pass. Spotting Gareth once more on the left wing, Russell sent the ball to him. Gareth, still rejoicing at playing a successful part in the last goal, once more transferred the ball to Jordan, unmarked by the careless Surfleet defence.

Jordan was perfectly happy to give a repeat performance of his skills, too. His speed carried him into the Surfleet penalty area before anyone could really move. This time the goalie remained on his line, but he was as helpless as a rabbit facing a stoat. Jordan leaned towards his left, the goalie started to move in that direction – and the ball entered the opposite corner of the net. Jordan had the knack of making goal-scoring look as easy as slicing up a sponge cake.

This time it was Gareth who led the rush to

embrace Dorlin's new hero; he either had not noticed, or chose to ignore, the green of Jordan's eyes. Tom, too, was ecstatic. His dreams of leading a winning side to the top of the League or to a Cup Final suddenly had a touch of reality. He knew that he himself couldn't have displayed such speed or close control of the ball at that pace.

The celebrations rather annoyed the referee. 'Come on, boys, it's only a game, you know,' he remarked loudly, waving them to their positions for the kick-off. Well, it was much more than that to most of the players, though no one risked saying so, in case the ref booked them for dissent or some other offence.

Surfleet re-organised immediately. Their fastest defender was ordered to attach himself to Dorlin's stick-thin striker like a postage stamp. He mustn't be allowed to run with freedom again. Someone else dropped back to provide extra cover – and the outcome of this new thinking was that from then on the Surfleet team stumbled and stuttered. Their free-flowing football just dried up. Dorlin, though they didn't realize it for a while, were no longer in danger. Even another own goal didn't upset them too much. Only Russell regarded it as a complete disaster . . .

Five

It happened just five minutes before full-time. By then, Dorlin were leading 3–0, the third goal having been scored by Tom from close-range following a free kick awarded when Jordan was fouled outside the penalty area soon after half-time. Surfleet were staging a final assault, striving to get something out of the match.

Their roly-poly playmaker for once decided to join the attack, something Dorlin hadn't expected. Defenders backed off, waiting for him to give the ball to a team-mate; and so he reached the edge of the penalty area without being tackled. Then, to everyone's surprise, he whipped the ball out to the left wing. The Surfleet winger took the ball neatly under control and raced towards goal at a sharp angle. Russell hesitated; should he stay where he was, close to the near post, or go out and tackle the raider? Quickly he glanced towards William, who was still on his line, waiting for the next move. Then, without slowing down or giving any hint of

what he intended, the attacker suddenly hit a fierce shot at goal.

The ball was still rising when it struck Russell on the head. But because it was going so fast he wasn't able to turn his neck to direct it away from goal. The ball glanced off his forehead, went into a perfect arc and then fell into the far top corner of the net – totally beyond William's reach, even if he had moved. He didn't: he remained, like a rooted tree, on his line.

It was, in a way, a comic sort of goal, but no one actually laughed; only the Surfleet winger who'd struck the shot was full of glee, because he intended to claim the goal. William, shaking his head in disbelief, went off to retrieve the ball. Tom just shrugged, knowing that the own goal wouldn't make any real difference to the result.

But Russell felt dreadful again. He'd spun round the moment the ball flew off him, expecting to see William catch it or another team-mate head it to safety. It would have been bad enough if a Surfleet player had scored; but for Russell himself to put the ball into his own net *again* was the worst thing he could imagine. It probably meant he was now playing his last game for Dorlin Tigers.

He didn't know how he got through the

remaining minutes; it felt as if he counted every second. All the time he was praying the ball wouldn't come anywhere near him, and perhaps his prayers were answered, because he didn't touch the ball again before the final whistle.

Russell was the only Dorlin player who didn't join in the celebrations.

'Tom, I'm terribly sorry . . . I mean, I'd no idea . . .'

'Oh, forget it,' the skipper said with a smile. 'We won, didn't we? That's what matters.'

'Yes, but if I hadn't . . .' Russell's voice trailed away in misery.

'Look, you got us a new player. Jordan's two goals against your own goal means, well, you're on the winning side, OK?'

Russell wanted to explain that he couldn't take credit for Jordan's goals; it was his own error he wanted to talk about. But Tom wasn't listening. He'd gone across to rejoice in their victory with William.

Gareth found someone else to discuss his video with as they changed, and Russell was on his own until Jordan came to sit beside him.

'Not a bad game, that,' remarked Jordan, pulling on brown-and-yellow socks. 'If they're one of the best teams, then I should score a few more goals in this League. Don't think it's as good as the League in London. I might even score one with a back-header!'

'That's not funny! I didn't do it on purpose! You'd think . . .'

Jordan put his arm round him. 'Hey, forget it. Don't get uptight about one measly own goal. It's not important. That's what my dad says to my mum when something's unimportant – don't get uptight.'

'But you see, I just couldn't get out of the way of the ball this time.' Russell wasn't convinced by Jordan's attitude. 'I should've moved back or ducked or something, not just stood there like a – like a lamp-post!'

Jordan shook his head. 'That wasn't what you did wrong.'

Russell turned to him in surprise and saw that his new friend was quite serious. 'What was it then?'

'Listen, can you come to the fair tonight?' Jordan asked eagerly as he pulled on a sweater. 'My dad's home and he's taking me and he says he'll be glad for you to come too.'

'Well, er, I suppose so.' Russell had never been

48

to the famous local fair at night because his dad was always busy and his mum didn't like crowds. But surely they'd let him go with his friend's dad.

'Great!' exclaimed Jordan, jumping to his feet. 'We'll call for you at half-six, OK?'

'Yes – yes, but, Jordan, what was I doing wrong? About the goal, I mean?'

'Tell you tonight.'

Russell screwed up his eyes in despair and disappointment. He hated waiting for anything; he always liked to know exactly what was going to happen, to be able to plan for things. That was the beauty of his computer games: he could work out the future with plenty of confidence. He needed to know *now* what was wrong with his football.

But Jordan had gone, moving like the wind. So Russell would just have to wait.

Six

Russell was sure he was going to die. The Giant Galactic Diver was poised at the very summit of its climb. In a second, two seconds, it would plunge towards earth. Russell had already experienced one of its dives and now he knew what it meant when people say, 'I was scared to death!' He was scared to death – but also secretly loving every moment of the dizzying dive.

Whoosh! Down they swooped and at least half the passengers screamed with real or mock terror. Russell, looking down, saw Jordan's knuckles were white as he gripped the safety bar. Yet, when he glanced sideways, he could see that Jordan's green eyes were sparkling with delight.

'Fantastic, wasn't it?' Jordan exclaimed when at last the ride was over.

Russell nodded, unable for the moment to speak. His stomach seemed to have a life of its own and was bouncing up and down inside him. At one point he was sure he was going to be sick, but somehow the feeling passed.

'Well, after that, how about a drink?' Mr Hall suggested. Jordan's father was plainly enjoying the fair as much as the boys. Wearing a red-and-white baseball cap bearing the message 'Have a Go, Go, GO!' he was joining in most things and paying for just about everything, even though Russell said he'd brought his own money with him.

'Hey, what I fancy is a nutburger,' Jordan said, pointing to a nearby stall from which clouds of steam and delicious smells were wafting towards them on this cool and breezy night. 'Oh, and a Coke'll go well with that. Thanks, Dad.'

'Russell, how about you?'

'Er, well, yes, thanks,' replied Russell, trying to decide if his stomach was stable again. Mr Hall went off to place the order.

'Honestly, Jordan, you never stop eating,' Russell remarked to his friend. 'Where does it all go? You're as thin as a pin!'

Jordan grinned. 'Very sharp of you to notice. I burn it up – food gives me bags of energy but I use it up pretty fast, especially running. My dad says I've got just the right system for playing sport.'

'Oh, listen, about my goal,' Russell started to say – but had to stop when Mr Hall handed him a nutburger and urged him to eat while it was still hot. It was so tasty, much tastier than Russell would have believed from its name, that he no longer gave a thought to his unsettled stomach. Jordan, who hadn't heard a word Russell said, was hunting for their next entertainment. He pointed to the dodgem cars.

'Hey, we've got to go on those,' he said excitedly. 'We can have three cars, can't we, Dad?'

'W-e-l-l, there's a lot of people waiting for cars, I think,' was the answer. 'You and Russell get in the first one and I'll try and grab another if I can.'

The music from the loudspeakers matched the crash-bang-thud-squeaks-and-screams from colliding cars and hysterical passengers. Then, abruptly, it stopped. The cars slowed down, slithering to a halt in a massive traffic jam.

'Let's go!' Jordan yelled, grabbing Russell by the arm and sprinting across the metal surface of the rink towards a red-and-yellow machine he'd had his eye on. Fortunately, driver and passenger were clambering out instead of staying on for another go.

'You can drive this one,' Jordan said generously. Russell, who'd never driven a dodgem car in his life, wasn't even sure how to do it until he found the pedal for the power on the floor. When he looked round again he got a wave from Mr Hall, who hadn't been lucky enough to seize a car.

The boy leaping from car to car collecting the money gave a thumbs-up sign to the man in charge. Music blared again, and, without warning, Russell found that their car was gliding forward. Everyone else, too, was on the move, beginning to jockey for a position in what was supposed to be a one-way circuit round the rink.

'Go for him, go for him!' Jordan yelled, pointing at a man in a blue-and-silver car, a man so large he seemed to be spilling out of the vehicle. But before Russell could react, they themselves received a shuddering thump from the rear that caused their car to slither sideways. Russell turned in time to see a fiendish grin on the face of another driver who, having rammed them, was now looking for another victim. Russell tried to steer the car into a space but another bumper caught them amidships and spun them round almost in a circle.

Russell fought for control but the car seemed to have stopped. 'Put your foot down!' Jordan instructed. 'It won't go without power. Go on, we're in a right jam here.'

With a twist of the wheel and foot flat down,

Russell managed to get the car moving, only to be hit again, this time head-on. To his amazement, Russell saw it was the boy with the fiendish grin who'd arrowed in on them again. Plainly he thought they were impossible to miss, so he was going to bash them as often as possible.

Jordan reached across to spin the wheel. 'We've got to get away from him, get our own back,' he said calmly.

Russell took charge again and aimed for a space between two cars that were just trundling around and avoiding contact with anyone, testing their skills by keeping out of any trouble at all. But before he could join them another pirate struck them a glancing blow, pushing them to one side, and by the time Russell could steer properly again the gap had gone.

'Look, just relax,' Jordan advised. 'Take what comes, sure, but give it back, twice as hard. You can't *plan* things in dodgems, you've got to react. And have fun! So let's get somebody – that fat guy's right behind us. Let him pass and then ram him!'

Russell thought *that* sounded like planning, of a kind, but he wasn't going to argue. He agreed that it was their turn to cause a bit of chaos. His target became the boy with the fiendish grin, who was driving with plenty of skill. He was going to take some catching, because his scarlet car really seemed faster than the rest.

'I know we're supposed to go round one way but nobody does,' Jordan yelled. 'So hit him over there!'

He was pointing to a boy about their age who was caught between two cars like cheese in a sandwich. Obediently Russell went for him, though he was such a soft target it hardly seemed fair. All the same, he laughed aloud when he smacked into the trapped car – and then deftly spun the wheel to drive clear of the pile-up.

'I'm getting the hang of this,' he said excitedly. At that moment, the car lost its momentum and everyone around them slid to a halt. Their time was up.

'Don't get out,' Jordan said. 'Dad'll give us another go so I can drive.'

Sure enough Mr Hall, already running to claim a car for himself, signalled to them to stay put. Russell couldn't help wishing that his own dad would share in a night like this. It was one of the best times he'd had for ages. *Almost* as good, he told himself, as playing soccer – in matches where he didn't score against his own side. He couldn't put those disasters out of his mind and he hoped Jordan had something useful to say about what was going wrong for him.

Suddenly, Jordan was out and running, yelling to Russell, 'Come on, come on!' He hurled himself into a car that dazzled with its black-and-gold wavy lines. 'Saw this one was free so I took a chance,' he explained to a startled Russell. 'Noticed it was pretty fast.'

The second the power was on, Jordan went in pursuit of his dad. With a goal-scorer's aim he rammed the rear of Mr Hall's slow car and got the response, 'Just you wait, Jordan. I'll get my own back.' But he didn't. Weaving in and out of the tide of traffic, Jordan scored plenty of hits and was hardly bumped by anyone. His dad kept turning this way and that to get on Jordan's tail, but Jordan's knack of darting into space kept them clear of trouble. Russell could only sit and admire his friend's talents.

'Well, that was just great, terrific.' Jordan was really glowing with pleasure as they strolled away from the dodgems at last. 'Wish we had one of those in our garden. I'd never have time for anything else.'

Russell decided this was the moment to ask his vital question. 'Look, Jordan, I must know: what did I do wrong when I, er, headed that own goal?'

'You thought their attacker was going to keep coming in, didn't you?'

Russell nodded. 'Yes, but what was wrong with that?'

'So you just hung around, waiting, doing nothing. Instead, you should have gone right at him, tackled him, or tried to. A goal wouldn't have happened if you'd done that. He'd have swerved or passed or something. *You* would have been in charge then, not him.'

Russell pondered that point of view. He didn't think he agreed with it, though. 'But I was sure he was going to keep coming in,' he pointed out. 'I wanted to prevent him having a chance of a shot. I didn't think he'd shoot from there . . . well, I mean, I don't know whether he was shooting or just trying to centre the ball.'

'But that's what you're doing wrong, Russ,' Jordan said fiercely, turning to face him. 'You're trying to work things out in advance, trying to out-*think* your opponent.'

He paused and then went on: 'Football's not like that. You don't have time for a lot of thinking and planning. The ball moves around so fast you just have to *react* to what's happening. Soccer isn't like chess, you know. You can't spend hours – well, ages – planning a move. You've got to get in there right away, either to stop them or to start something going for us. Really, it's more like the dodgems. If you don't attack, you get bashed up. There's no time for clever thinking, Russ.'

'What on earth are you going on about, Jordan?' asked his dad, rejoining them after trying to win a prize at darts. 'What don't you need to be clever at?'

'Football, that's what we're talking about,' his son answered promptly.

Mr Hall groaned like an actor in a pantomime. 'I might have guessed. Listen, you're supposed to be having a night off football. For goodness' sake, let's think of something else. Tell you what, we'll go and watch the Wall of Death. That'll take your mind off football.'

It didn't succeed in taking Russell's mind off the subject. Even the sight of motorbikes being ridden round the inside walls of a circular wooden structure didn't capture all his attention, thrilling though it was. The other spectators, peering down from the high platform, were wondering whether the daring riders would fall off as they zoomed up and down the walls like human flies on two wheels. All Russell could think of was how to avoid scoring own goals. If he failed, he'd surely be dropped from Dorlin Tigers for ever.

Seven

As always, Tiger Tom knew what he wanted. 'I want you to be as careful as a juggler on a tight-rope,' he told Russell. (The previous night Tom had been to a circus.) 'We're moving up the League table so I don't want us sliding down any snakes.' (He had also developed a passion for snakes and ladders.)

'I know,' said Russell. He certainly knew that the match against Cove Hill Raiders was very, very important to Dorlin Tigers. For most of the week, he'd feared he wouldn't be in the team, but the captain had just told him he was giving him a last chance.

'Good,' said Tom, briskly. 'I don't want to lose you, Russ, but I can't have anybody in the team who keeps scoring own goals.'

'I know,' Russell said again. It had crossed his mind that the skipper wasn't helping his confidence by reminding him of his mistakes. If he, Russell, had been captain, he'd have told an unhappy culprit to forget what had happened and just do his best in the next match. Tom had a different approach to leading a team.

The Raiders were the sort of team who might do anything, lose heavily or fight for every ball and give nothing away, snatching victory with almost the last kick of the match. They possessed some very clever players, but team-mates often got angry with each other or sulked after making an error, or risked being sent off for violent conduct. Russell naturally hoped they were in a mood to give in easily and present the Tigers with the three easy points needed for a win.

Ever since his talk at the fair with Jordan he had been thinking how he could improve his play. So far, though, he hadn't been able to work out a course of action. Like Tom's tightrope juggler, he would just have to take one step at a time and try not to think too far ahead. If he failed again, then he'd better give up football and turn to something else. But he couldn't bear that . . .

Wearing their usual strip of black shorts and white shirts with a single red stripe across the chest, the Raiders came out of their changing room in a rush, as if about to take part in a mass sprint race. Russell noted with some alarm that, as a bunch, their forwards looked big and strong; he hoped they weren't also fast.

Jordan had a different view: 'Don't look as if they know much about soccer – they're bashing the ball everywhere. We'll beat them, no danger.' He was warming up by firing shots at William, who was casting anxious looks at the Cove Hill side as if he shared Russell's thoughts.

Within moments of the kick-off their worries were justified. In their first attack the Raiders did their best to knock William into the back of his own net! When he went up to collect a high centre, their biggest striker hurled himself bodily at the goal-keeper. As he hit the ground William lost control of the ball, which ran loose for the striker to belt it joyfully into the back of the net. He even thought he'd scored a real goal. The referee was a boy not much older than the players, but he wasn't going to tolerate that nonsense. He gave the culprit a stern lecture and a warning that, if it were repeated, he'd be sent off. The player grumbled but the sight of a yellow card at last silenced him.

William limped away from the scene, his face screwed up in pain. Tom had a word with him but the goalkeeper said he wanted to stay on the pitch, even though his knee hurt badly. One of the linesmen – who was actually a girl training to be a referee – came on to see to the injury carrying a medical bag. With short, strong fingers she probed and prodded William's knee, and Russell thought she looked worried.

'I'm not sure how bad it is,' she told him, applying the pain-killing spray. 'If it feels bad again, let me know. We mustn't risk more damage.'

'Thanks, Vicky,' said the referee before blowing his whistle for a free kick to be taken by Russell. One of their players being booked didn't appear to worry the Raiders or affect the way they played. In their next attack Russell was the one who was hacked down, but he didn't suffer any injury. Again the referee brought out the yellow card and then spoke to the Cove Hill captain. 'This is a football field, not a *battle*field. If you don't get a grip on your players I shall – and you'll all suffer.'

For the next few minutes there was no trouble at all. Then the Tigers scored, and that really upset their opponents. It was Jordan's lightning speed that brought about the goal. He moved so fast to take a pass from Gareth that the Raiders protested he was offside when he received the ball. But no whistle sounded and so Jordan sped away through the defence to the edge of the penalty area. The

64

goalkeeper parried the shot but couldn't hold it. And Tom, following up, slid the ball into the net.

'Nothing offside there,' the referee told the protestors. 'Don't forget, boys, I'm the one who makes the decisions.'

Desperate to get the equalizer, the Raiders poured players into the attack and succeeded in winning a corner. William went up to take the ball as it came over but when he was knocked over he didn't get up again, although he clung to the ball. While Vicky – the helpful linesgirl – ran on to attend to poor, battered William, the referee flourished the red card. The culprit tried to argue he wasn't at fault, the Cove Hill skipper got a booking for muttering some dreadful words, and the ref announced he'd send off more players if necessary.

'I'm afraid you'll have to come off,' Vicky told William, whose face was now drawn. 'This knee needs proper attention. But for the present you must rest it.'

'But who'll take my place in goal?' asked the worried William, looking at Tom.

The captain glanced at his players in turn and then his eyes rested on Russell. Suddenly sensing what was in Tom's mind, Russell looked away.

He'd hate playing in goal – it would be almost as bad as scoring against his own team.

'Russell, I think you'd be our best stand-in goalie,' Tom declared in a firm voice. 'So just swap shirts with William, OK?'

'But – but – but why can't our sub play in goal?' Russell asked desperately. 'I mean, I've never been in goal in my life.'

'Matthew is a natural full-back, so he can take your place.' Tom replied. 'And I think you'll try your best to be a great goalkeeper. Look, hurry up. We've got to get on with the game.'

'I was just going to say the same,' added Vicky. Having helped William to take off his red jersey and pull on Russell's shirt, she guided him to the touchline, where a spectator wrapped him in his own anorak.

Russell, who'd never suspected that Matthew was any kind of defender, dragged on the jersey, wondering how long it was to half-time. During the interval he might be able to persuade Tom to put someone else in goal for the remainder of the match. For the moment, though, he had to make sure he didn't commit some ghastly error and let the team down. Tom was absolutely right: he *would* try his hardest to be a capable goalkeeper. At least we're winning, he told himself – and they're down to ten men.

The loss of their biggest striker didn't seem to worry Cove Hill. They pushed someone else up front to take his place and launched another attack. The ball was switched to the right wing and then almost immediately punted back into the middle, towards the penalty area. A Raider picked it up, swept past the slow moving Matthew and headed for goal, pushing the ball well ahead of him. Russell didn't hesitate. The threat was plain, and no one was giving him any cover.

Sprinting from his line, he flung himself at the ball, not taking his eye off it for an instant. He reached it a split-second before the Raider's boot and pulled it into his chest before his opponent could get a second chance of a kick. Then, calmly, he got to his feet, bounced the ball a couple of times and booted it up-field. Tom, he saw, was nodding at him and clapping with his hands above his head. Russell grinned. His first save as a goalkeeper was a success!

Before half-time he handled the ball twice more, once jumping out to take a high cross and then, as Matthew dithered, calling for a back-pass and getting it.

'Terrific,' Tom told him at the break. 'You look just as safe as William does when you go for the ball. You're a natural, honestly.'

Russell knew there couldn't be higher praise from Tiger Tom, William's best friend. However, it also meant he was unlikely to agree to Russell giving up the job as goalie. By now William himself had been taken home by a parent who'd just arrived to watch the match. The easiest thing, therefore, was for Russell to keep the red jersey on.

So far goalkeeping hadn't proved to be as bad as he'd feared. There wasn't time to think about problems. He'd seen what had to be done – and he'd done it. Done it *immediately*, and skilfully. It was proving easier to follow Jordan's advice in goal than it was in mid-field.

Things didn't seem to change much in the second half. The Raiders continued to raid and Russell continued to defy them, diving, punching, jumping, catching. At one point he grazed a knee but waved Vicky away when she offered to treat it. Cove Hill threw everything they could at him but couldn't force the ball past him.

Then, with only two minutes of the match left, Matthew handled the ball in the penalty area. In spite of playing against only ten men, the Dorlin

Tigers hadn't managed to add to their single goal. So now Cove Hill only needed to score from the penalty spot to get a point from the match.

Tom ran up to his goalkeeper. 'I've no idea where he'll aim,' he said, 'so just do your best. Good luck!'

Russell, licking his lips and looking round, saw that Jordan was signalling that he had his fingers crossed for him – and for the Tigers. Should he dive to the left or to the right? He stared at the penalty-taker, another tall, strongly built boy. He'd have a kick like a mule, thought Russell.

His eyes never left the ball: he watched it as the

kicker ran in; he watched it rise from the spot; he watched it flash towards the top of his net to the left. Until he knew where it was going he never moved. And then he leapt – and pushed – and deflected the ball high over the cross-bar for a corner kick. Russell had saved the first penalty kick he'd ever faced.

'Brilliant, brilliant!' Tom exclaimed, dashing up to pat him on the back. Nobody had ever seen the captain of Dorlin Tigers so excited. But there wasn't time for everyone to congratulate the team's saviour because Cove Hill were rushing to take the corner kick.

They needn't have bothered. Russell collected the ball effortlessly when it floated over and punted it away to set up the Tigers' final attack. Jordan took a pass near the edge of the penalty area and, seeing the Raiders' goalkeeper well off his line, hit the ball beyond him and into the net. There was no time for anything else to happen and so the Tigers won 2–0.

With his new striker on one side of him and his new goalkeeper on the other, Tom left the pitch in the happiest of moods, already looking forward to the next match.

'Look, you will stay in goal for us, won't you?' he

asked Russell. 'I mean, William's always wanted to play in mid-field. Oh, and Matthew will get better with you behind him. Honestly, Russ, you're a natural as a goalie.'

'Well, I did enjoy it today,' Russell admitted. 'I just watched the ball, that's all. It was great not having to plan everything. I don't know if I want to be in goal for *every* match, Tom. But, OK, I'll have a go in the next match as well.'

'That's it,' Jordan grinned. 'Just take each shot as it comes.'